WHILE THE SMOKE ROLLED

BY

ROBERT E. HOWARD

British Library Cataloguing-in-Publication Data
A catalogue record for this book is available from the
British Library

Robert E. Howard

Robert Ervin Howard was born in Peaster, Texas in 1906. During his youth, his family moved between a variety of Texan boomtowns, and Howard – a bookish and somewhat introverted child – was steeped in the violent myths and legends of the Old South. Although he loved reading and learning, Howard developed a distinctly Texan, hardboiled outlook on the world. He became a passionate fan of boxing, taking it up at an amateur level, and from the age of nine began to write adventure tales of semi-historical bloodshed. In 1919, when Howard was thirteen, his family moved to the Central Texas hamlet of Cross Plains, where he would stay for the rest of his life.

At fifteen Howard began to read the pulp magazines of the day, and to write more seriously. The December 1922 issue of his high school newspaper featured two of his stories, 'Golden Hope Christmas' and 'West is West'. In 1924 he sold his first piece – a short caveman tale titled 'Spear and Fang' – for $16 to the not-yet-famous *Weird Tales* magazine. He published with the magazine regularly over the next few years. 1929 was a breakout year for Howard, in that the 23-year-old writer began to sell to other magazines, such as *Ghost Stories* and *Argosy,* both of whom had previously sent him hundreds of rejection slips. In 1930, he began a correspondence with weird fiction master H. P. Lovecraft which ran up to his death six years later, and is regarded as one of the great correspondence cycles in all of fantasy literature.

It was partly due to Lovecraft's encouragement that Howard created his most famous character, Conan the Cimmerian. Conan – a barbarian-turned-King during the Hyborian Age, a mythical period of some 12,000 years ago – featured in seventeen *Weird Tales* stories between 1933 and 1936, and is now regarded as having spawned the 'sword and sorcery' genre, making Howard's influence on fantasy literature comparable to that of J. R. R. Tolkien's. The Conan stories have since been adapted many times, most famously in the series of films starring Arnold Schwarzenegger.

Howard was enjoying an all-time high in sales by the beginning of 1936, but he was also deeply upset by the ill health of his mother, who had fallen into a coma. On the morning of June 11, 1936, he asked an attending nurse whether she would ever recover, and the nurse replied negatively. Howard walked to his car, parked outside the family home in Cross Plains, and shot himself. He died eight hours later, aged just thirty.

"The War of 1812 might have had a very different ending if Sir Wilmot Pembroke had succeeded in his efforts to organize the Western Indians into one vast confederacy to hurl against the American frontier; just why he did fail is as great a mystery as is the nature of the accident which forced his companions to carry him back to Canada on a stretcher."

--Wilkinson's "History of the Northwest."

Wolf Mountain, Texas. March 10, 1879 Mister WN. Wilkinson. Chicago, Illinoy.

Dear Sir:

The schoolmarm down to Coon Creek was reading the above passage to me out of yore history book which you writ. It ain't no mystery. It's all explained in this here letter which I'm sending you which has been sticking in the family Bible along with the birth records for years. It was writ by my grandpap. Please send it back when you've read it, and oblige.

Yores respeckfully.

Pike Bearfield, Esquire.

* * * *

Aboard the keelboat Pirut Queen. On the Missoury. September, 1814. Mister Peter Bearfield. Nashville, Tennessee.

Dear Sir:

Well, pap, I hope you air satisfied, perswading me to stay out here on the Missoury and skin bufflers and fight musketeers, whilst everybody else in the family is having big doings and enjoying theirselves. When I think about Bill and John and Joel marching around with Gen'ral Hickory Jackson, and wearing them gorgeous unerforms, and fighting in all them fine battles yore having back there I could dang near bawl. I ain't going to be put on no more jest because I'm the youngest. Soon's I git back to Saint Louis I'm going to throw up my job and head for Tennessee, and the Missoury Fur Company can go to hell. I ain't going to spend all my life working for a living whilst my wuthless brothers has all the fun, by golly, I ain't. And if you tries to oppress me any more, I'll go and enlist up North and git to be a Yankee; you can see from this how desprut I be, so you better consider.

Anyway, I jest been through a experience up beyond Owl River which has soured me on the whole dern fur trade. I reckon you'll say what the hell has he been doing up the river this time of year, there ain't no furs up there in the summer. Well, it was all on account of Big Nose, the Minnetaree chief, and I git sick at my stummick right now every time I see a Minnetaree.

You know the way the guvment takes Injun chiefs East and shows 'em the cities and forts and armies and things. The idea being that the chief will git so scairt when he sees how strong the white man is, that when he gits home he won't never go on the war-path no more. So he comes home and tells the tribe about what he seen, and they accuse him of being a liar and say he's been bought off by the white folks; so he gits mad and goes out and sculps the first white man he meets jest to demonstrate his independence. But it's a good theery, anyway.

So they taken Big Nose to Memphis and would of took him all the way to Washington, only they was scairt they'd run into a battle somewheres on the way and the cannon would scare Big Nose into a decline. So they brung him back to Saint Charles and left him for the company to git him back to his village on Knife River. So Joshua Humphrey, one of the clerks, he put a crew of twenty men and four hunters onto the Pirut Queen, and loaded Big Nose on, and we started. The other three hunters was all American too, and the boatmen was Frenchies from down the Mississippi.

I wisht you could of saw Big Nose. He had on a plug hat they give him, and a blue swaller-tailed coat with brass buttons, and a big red sash and broadcloth britches--only he'd cut the seat out of 'em like a Injun always does; and the boots they give him hurt his flat feet, so he wore 'em tied around his neck. He was the most pecooliar-looking critter I ever laid eyes onto, and I shuddered to think what'd happen when the Sioux first ketched sight of him. Big Nose shuddered too, and more'n I did, because the Sioux hated him anyhow, and the Tetons had swore to kiver a drum with his hide.

But all the way up the Lower River he was like a hawg in clover, because the Omahas and Osages and Iowas would come down to the bank and look at him, clap their hands over their open mouths to show how astonished and admireful they was. He strutted and swelled all over the boat. But the further away from the Platte we got the more his feathers drooped; and one day a Injun rode up on the bluffs and looked at us as we went past, and he was a Sioux. Big Nose had a chill and we had to revive him with about a quart of company rum, and it plumb broke my heart to see all that good licker going to waste down a Injun's gullet. When Big Nose come to, he shed his white man's duds and got into his regular outfit--which was mostly a big red blanket that looked like a prairie fire by sunset. I told Joshua he better throw the blanket overboard, because it was knowed all up and down the river, and any Sioux would recognize it at a glance. But Joshua said if we threw it overboard we'd have to throw Big Nose overboard too, because he thought it was big medicine. Anyway, he said, they warn't no use trying to keep the Sioux from knowing we was taking Big Nose home. They knowed it already and would take him away from us if they could. Joshua said he aimed to use diplomacy to save Big Nose's sculp. I didn't like the sound of that, because I notice when somebody I'm working for uses diplomacy it generally means I got to risk my neck and he gits the credit. Jest like you, pap, when you git to working and figgering, like you say, the way it always comes around you do the figgering and I do the working.

The further north we got, the closter Big Nose stayed in the cabin which ain't big enough to swing a cat in; but Big Nose didn't want to swing no cat, and every time he come on deck he seen swarms of Sioux all over the bluffs jest fixing for to descent on him. Joshua said it was hallucernations, but I said it would be delirium trimmings purty soon if that jug warn't took away from him.

We made purty good time, ten to twenty miles a day, except when we had winds agen us, or had to haul the boat along on the cordelle--which is a big line that the Frenchies gits out and pulls on, in case you don't know. Towing a twenty-ton keelboat in water up to yore neck ain't no joke.

Every day we expected trouble with the Sioux, but we got past the mouth of the Owl River all right, and Joshua said he guessed the Sioux knowed better'n to try any monkey business with him. And that very day a Yankton on a piebald hoss hailed us from the bluffs, and told us they was a hundred Tetons laying in ambush for us amongst the willers along the next p'int of land. We'd have to go around it on the cordelle; and whilst the boatmen was tugging and hauling in water up to their waists, the Sioux aimed to jump us. The Yankton said the Tetons didn't have nothing personal agen us white men, and warn't aiming to do us no harm--outside of maybe cutting our throats for a joke--but you oughta herd what he said they was going to do to Big Nose. It war plumb scandalous.

Big Nose ducked down into the cabin and started having another chill; and the Frenchies got scairt and would of turnt the boat around and headed for Saint Charles if we'd let 'em. Us hunters wanted Joshua to put us ashore and let us circle the p'int from inland and come onto the Sioux from behind. We could do a sight of damage to 'em before they knowed we was onto 'em. But Joshua said not even four American hunters could lick a hundred Sioux, and he furthermore said shet up and let him think. So he sot down on a kag and thunk for a spell, and then he says to me: "Ain't Fat Bear's village out acrost yonder about five mile?"

I said yes, and he said: "Well, look, you put on Big Nose's blanket and git on the Yankton's hoss and head for the village. The Sioux'll think we've throwed Big Nose out to root for hisself; and whilst they're chasin' you the boat can git away up the river with Big Nose."

"I don't suppose it matters what happens to me!" I says bitterly.

"Oh," says he, "Fat Bear is yore friend and wunst you git in his village he won't let the Sioux git you. You'll have a good start before they can see you, on account of the bluffs there, and you ought to be able to beat 'em into the village."

"I suppose it ain't occurred to you at all that they'll shott arrers at me all the way," I says.

"You know a Sioux cain't shoot as good from a runnin' hoss as a Comanche can," he reassured me. "You jest keep three or four hundred yards ahead of 'em, and I bet they won't hit you hardly any at all."

"Well, why don't you do it, then?" I demanded.

At this Joshua bust into tears. "To think that you should turn agen me after all I've did for you!" he wept--though what he ever done for me outside of trying to skin me out of my wages I dunno. "After I taken you off'n a Natchez raft and persuaded the company to give you a job at a princely salary, you does this to me! A body'd think you didn't give a dern about my personal safety! My pore old grandpap used to say: 'Bewar' of a Southerner like you would a hawk! He'll eat yore vittles and drink yore licker and then stick you with a butcher knife jest to see you kick!' When I thinks--"

"Aw, hesh up," I says in disgust. "I'll play Injun for you. I'll put on the blanket and stick feathers in my hair, but I'll be derned if I'll cut the seat out a my britches."

"It'd make it look realer," he argued, wiping his eyes on the fringe of my hunting shirt.

"Shet up!" I yelled with passion. "They is a limit to everything!"

"Oh, well, all right," says he, "if you got to be temperamental. You'll have the blanket on over yore pants, anyway."

So we went into the cabin to git the blanket, and would you believe me, that derned Injun didn't want to lemme have it, even when his fool life was at stake. He thought it was a medicine blanket, and the average Injun would ruther lose his life than his medicine. In fack, he give us a tussle for it, and they is no telling how long it would of went on if he hadn't accidentally banged his head agen a empty rum bottle I happened to have in my hand at the time. It war plumb disgusting. He also bit me severely in the hind laig, whilst I was setting on him and pulling the feathers out of his hair-- which jest goes to show how much gratitude a Injun has got. But Joshua said the company had contracted to deliver him to Hidatsa, and we was going to do it if we had to kill him.

Joshua give the Yankton a hatchet and a blanket, and three shoots of powder for his hoss--which was a awful price- -but the Yankton knowed we had to have it and gouged us for all it was wuth. So I put on the red blanket, and stuck the feathers in my hair, and got on the hoss, and started up a gully for the top of the bluffs. Joshua yelled: "If you git to the village, stay there till we come back down the river. We'll pick you up then. I'd be doin' this myself, but it wouldn't be right for me to leave the boat. T'wouldn't be fair to the company money to replace it, and--"

"Aw, go to hell!" I begged, and kicked the piebald in the ribs and headed for Fat Bear's village.

When I got up on the bluffs, I could see the p'int; and the Sioux seen me and was fooled jest like Joshua said, because they come b'iling out of the willers and piled onto their ponies and lit out after me. Their hosses was better'n mine, jest as I suspected, but I had a good start; and I was still ahead of 'em when we topped a low ridge and got within sight of Fat Bear's village--which was, so far as I know, the only Arikara village south of Grand River. I kept expectin' a arrer in my back because they was within range now, and their howls was enough to freeze a mortal's blood; but purty soon I realized that they aimed to take me alive. They thought I was Big Nose, and they detested him so thorough a arrer through the back was too good for him. So I believed I had a good chance of making it after all, because I seen the piebald was going to last longer'n the Tetons thought he would.

I warn't far from the village now, and I seen that the tops of the lodges was kivered with Injuns watching the race. Then a trade-musket cracked, and the ball whistled so clost it stang my ear, and all to wunst I remembered that Fat Bear didn't like Big Nose no better'n the Sioux did. I could see him up on his lodge taking aim at me again, and the Sioux was right behind me. I was in a hell of a pickle. If I taken the blanket off and let him see who I was, the Sioux would see I warn't Big Nose, too, and fill me full of arrers; and if

I kept the blanket on he'd keep on shooting at me with his cussed gun.

Well, I'd ruther be shot at by one Arikara than a hundred Sioux, so all I could do was hope he'd miss. And he did, too; that is he missed me, but his slug taken a notch out of the piebald's ear, and the critter r'ared up and throwed me over his head; he didn't have no saddle nor bridle, jest a hackamore. The Sioux howled with glee and their chief, old Bitin' Hoss, he was ahead of the others; and he rode in and grabbed me by the neck as I riz.

I'd lost my rifle in the fall, but I hit Bitin' Hoss betwixt the eyes with my fist so hard I knocked him off'n his hoss and I bet he rolled fifteen foot before he stopped. I grabbed for his hoss, but the critter bolted, so I shucked that blanket and pulled for the village on foot. The Sioux was so surprized to see Big Nose turn into a white man they forgot to shoot at me till I had run more'n a hundred yards; and then when they did let drive, all the arrers missed but one. It hit me right where you kicked Old Man Montgomery last winter and I will have their heart's blood for it if it's the last thing I do. You jest wait; the Sioux nation will regret shooting a Bearfield behind his back. They come for me lickety-split but I had too good a start; they warn't a hoss in Dakota could of ketched me under a quarter of a mile.

The Arikaras was surprized too, and some of 'em fell off their tipis and nearly broke their necks. They was too stunned to open the gate to the stockade, so I opened it myself--hit it with my shoulder and knocked it clean off'n the rawhide hinges and fell inside on top of it. The Sioux was almost on top of me, with their arrers drawed back, but now they sot their hosses back onto their haunches and held their fire. If they'd come in after me it would of meant a fight with the Arikaras. I half expected 'em to come in anyway, because the Sioux ain't no ways scairt of the Arikaras, but in a minute I seen why they didn't.

Fat Bear had come down off of his lodge, and I riz up and says: "Hao!"

"Hao!" says he, but he didn't say it very enthusiastic. He's a fat-bellied Injun with a broad, good-natured face; and outside of being the biggest thief on the Missouri, he's a good friend of the white men--especially me, because I wunst taken him away from the Cheyennes when they was going to burn him alive.

Then I seen about a hundred strange braves in the crowd, and they was Crows. I recognized their chief, old Spotted Hawk, and I knowed why the Sioux didn't come in after me in spite of the Arikaras. That was why Fat Bear was a chief, too. A long time ago he made friends with Spotted Hawk, and when the Sioux or anybody crowded him too clost, the Crows would come in and help him. Them Crows air scrappers and no mistake.

15

"This is plumb gaudy!" I says. "Git yore braves together and us and the Crows will go out and run them fool Tetons clean into the Missoury, by golly."

"No, no, no!" says he. He's hung around the trading posts till he can talk English nigh as good as me. "There's a truce between us! Big powwow tonight!"

Well, the Sioux knowed by now how they'd been fooled; but they also knowed the Pirut Queen would be past the p'int and outa their reach before they could git back to the river; so they camped outside, and Bitin' Hoss hollered over the stockade: "There is bad flesh in my brother's village! Send it forth that we may cleanse it with fire!"

Fat Bear bust into a sweat and says: "That means they want to bum you! Why did you have to come here, jest at this time?"

"Well," I says in a huff, "air you goin' to hand me over to 'em?"

"Never!" says he, wiping his brow with a bandanner he stole from the guvment trading post below the Kansas. "But I'd rather a devil had come through that gate than a Big Knife!" That's what them critters calls a American. "We and the Crows and Sioux have a big council on tonight, and--"

Jest then a man in a gilded cock hat and a red coat come through the crowd, with a couple of French Canadian trappers, and a pack of Soc Injuns from the Upper Mississippi.

He had a sword on him and he stepped as proud as a turkey gobbler in the fall.

"What is this bloody American doing here?" says he, and I says: "Who the hell air you?" And he says: "Sir Wilmot Pembroke, agent of Indian affairs in North America for his Royal Majesty King George, that's who!"

"Well, step out from the crowd, you lobster-backed varmint," says I, stropping my knife on my leggin', "and I'll decorate a sculp-pole with yore innards--and that goes for them two Hudson Bay skunks, too!"

"No!" says Fat Bear, grabbing my arm. "There is a truce! No blood must be spilled in my village! Come into my lodge."

"The truce doesn't extend beyond the stockade," says Sir Wilmot. "Would you care to step outside with me?"

"So yore Teton friends could fill me with arrers?" I sneered. "I ain't as big a fool as I looks."

"No, that wouldn't be possible," agreed he, and I was so overcame with rage all I could do was gasp. Another instant and I would of had my knife in his guts, truce or no truce, but Fat Bear grabbed me and got me into his tipi. He had me set on a pile of buffler hides and one of his squaws brung me a pot of meat; but I was too mad to be hungry, so I only et four or five pounds of buffler liver.

Fat Bear sot down his trade musket, which he had stole from a Hudson Bay Company trapper, and said: "The council tonight is to decide whether or not the Arikaras shall take the warpath against the Big Knives. This Red-Coat, Sir Wilmot, says the Big White Chief over the water is whipping the Big White Father of the Big Knives, in the village called Washington."

I was so stunned by this news I couldn't say nothing. We hadn't had no chance to git news about the war since we started up the river.

"Sir Wilmot wants the Sioux, Crows and Arikaras to join him in striking the American settlements down the river," says Fat Bear. "The Crows believe the Big Knives are losing the war, and they're wavering. If they go with the Sioux, I must go too; otherwise the Sioux will burn my village. I cannot exist without the aid of the Crows. The Red-Coat has a Soc medicine man, who will go into a medicine lodge tonight and talk with the Great Spirit. It is big medicine, such was never seen before on any village on the Missouri. The medicine man will tell the Crows and the Arikaras to go with the Sioux."

"You mean this Englishman aims to lead a war-party down the river?" I says, plumb horrified.

"Clear to Saint Louis!" says Fat Bear. "He will wipe out all the Americans on the river!"

"He won't neither," says I with great passion, rising and drawing my knife. "I'll go over to his lodge right now and cut his gizzard out!"

But Fat Bear grabbed me and hollered: "If you spill blood, no one will ever dare recognize a truce again! I cannot let you kill the Red-Coat!"

"But he's plannin' to kill everybody on the river, dern it!" I yelled. "What'm I goin' to do?"

"You must get up in council and persuade the warriors not to go on the war-path," says he.

"Good gosh," I says, "I can't make no speech."

"The Red-Coat has a serpent's tongue," says Fat Bear, shaking his head. "If he had presents to give the chiefs, his cause would be as good as won. But his boat upset as he came along the river, and all his goods were lost. If you had presents to give to Spotted Hawk and Biting Horse--"

"You know I ain't got no presents!" I roared, nigh out of my head. "What the hell am I goin' to do?"

"I dunno," says he, despairful. "Some white men pray when they're in a pickle."

"I'll do it!" I says. "Git outa my way!" So I kneeled down on a stack of buffler robes, and I'd got as far as: "Now I lay me down to sleep--" when my knee nudged something under the hides that felt familiar. I reched down and yanked it out--and sure enough, it was a keg!

"Where'd you git this?" I yelped.

"I stole it out of the company's storehouse the last time I was in Saint Louis," he confessed, "but--"

"But nothin'!" exulted I. "I dunno how come you ain't drunk it all up before now, but it's my wampum! I ain't goin' to try to out-talk that lobster-back tonight. Soon's the council's open, I'll git up kind of casual and say that the Red-Coat has got a empty bag of talk for 'em, with nothin' to go with it, but the Big White Father at Washington has sent 'em a present. Then I'll drag out the keg. T'aint much to divide up amongst so many, but the chiefs is what counts, and they's enough licker to git them too drunk to know what Sir Wilmot and the medicine man says."

"They know you didn't bring anything into the village with you," he says.

"So much the better," I says. "I'll tell 'em it's wakan and I can perjuice whiskey out of the air."

"They'll want you to perjuice some more," says he.

"I'll tell 'em a evil spirit, in the shape of a skunk with a red coat on, is interferin' with my magic powers," I says, gitting brainier every minute. "That'll make 'em mad at Sir Wilmot. Anyway, they won't care where the licker come from. A few snorts and the Sioux will probably remember all the gredges they got agen the Socs and run 'em outa camp."

"You'll get us all killed," says Fat Bear, mopping his brow. "But about that keg, I want to tell you--"

"You shet up about that keg," I says sternly. "It warn't yore keg in the first place. The fate of a nation is at stake, and you tries to quibble about a keg of licker! Git some stiffenin' into yore laigs; what we does tonight may decide who owns this continent. If we puts it over it'll be a big gain for the Americans."

"And what'll the Indians get out of it?" he ast.

"Don't change the subjeck," I says. "I see they've stacked buffler hides out at the council circle for the chiefs and guests to get on--and by the way, you be dern sure you gives me a higher stack to get on than Sir Wilmot gits. When nobody ain't lookin', you hide this keg clost to where I'm to set. If I had to send to yore lodge to git it, it'd take time and look fishy, too."

"Well," he begun reluctantly, but I flourished a fist under his nose and said with passion: "Dang it, do like I says! One more blat outa you and I busts the truce and yore snoot simultaneous!"

So he spread his hands kinda helpless, and said something about all white men being crazy, and anyway he reckoned he'd lived as long as the Great Spirit aimed for him to. But I give no heed, because I have not got no patience with them Injun superstitions. I started out of his lodge and dang near fell over one of them French trappers which they called Ondrey; t'other'n was named Franswaw.

"What the hell you doin' here?" I demanded, but he merely give me a nasty look and snuck off. I started for the lodge where the Crows was, and the next man I met was old Shingis. I dunno what his real name is, we always call him old Shingis; I think he's a Iowa or something. He's so old he's done forgot where he was born, and so ornery he jest lives around with first one tribe and then another till they git tired of him and kick him out.

He ast for some tobaccer and I give him a pipe-full, and then he squinted his eye at me and said: "The Red-Coat did not have to bring a man from the Mississippi to talk with Waukontonka. They say Shingis is heyoka. They say he is a friend of the Unktehi, the Evil Spirits."

Well, nobody never said that but him, but that's the way Injuns brag on theirselves; so I told him everybody knowed he was wakan, and went on to the lodge where the Crows was. Spotted Hawk ast me if it was the Red-Coats had burnt Washington and I told him not to believe everything a Red-Coat told him. Then I said: "Where's this Red-Coat's presents?"

Spotted Hawk made a wry face because that was a p'int which stuck in his mind, too, but he said: "The boat upset and the river took the gifts meant for the chiefs."

"Then that means that the Unktehi air mad at him," I says. "His medicine's weak. Will you foller a man which his medicine is weak?"

"We will listen to what he has to say in council," says Spotted Hawk, kind of uncertain, because a Injun is scairt of having anything to do with a man whose medicine is weak.

It was gitting dark by this time, and when I come out of the lodge I met Sir Wilmot, and he says: "Trying to traduce the Crows, eh? I'll have the pleasure of watching my Sioux friends roast you yet! Wait till Striped Thunder talks to them from the medicine lodge tonight."

"He who laughs last is a stitch in time," I replied with dignerty, so tickled inside about the way I was going to put it over him I was reconciled to not cutting his throat. I then went on, ignoring his loud, rude laughter. Jest wait! thunk I, jest wait! Brains always wins in the end.

I passed by the place where the buffler hides had been piled in a circle, in front of a small tipi made out of white buffler skins. Nobody come nigh that place till the powwow opened, because it was wakan, as the Sioux say, meaning magic. But all of a sudden I seen old Shingis scooting through the tipis clostest to the circle, making a arful face. He grabbed a water bucket made out of a buffler's stummick, and drunk about a gallon, then he shook his fists and talked to hisself energetic. I said: "Is my red brother's heart pained?"

"#%&*@!" says old Shingis. "There is a man of black heart in this village! Let him beware! Shingis is the friend of the Unktehi!"

Then he lit out like a man with a purpose, and I went on to Fat Bear's lodge. He was squatting on his robes looking at hisself in a mirrer he stole from the Northwest Fur Company three seasons ago.

"What you doin'?" I ast, reching into the meat pot.

"Trying to imagine how I'll look after I'm scalped," says he. "For the last time, that keg--"

"Air you tryin' to bring that subjeck up agen?" I says, rising in wrath; and jest then a brave come to the door to say that everybody was ready to go set in council.

"See?" whispers Fat Bear to me. "I'm not even boss in my own village when Spotted Hawk and Biting Horse are here! They give the orders!"

We went to the powwow circle, which they had to hold outside because they warn't a lodge big enough to hold all of 'em. The Arikaras sot on one side, the Crows on the other and the Sioux on the other. I sot beside Fat Bear, and Sir Wilmot and his Socs and Frenchmen sot opposite us. The medicine man sot cross-legged, with a heavy wolf-robe over his shoulders--though it was hot enough to fry a aig, even after the sun had went down. But that's the way a heyoka man does. If it'd been snowing, likely he'd of went naked. The women and chillern got up on top of the lodges to watch us, and I whispered and ast Fat Bear where the keg was. He said under the robes right behind me. He then started humming his death-song under his breath.

I begun feeling for it, but before I found it, Sir Wilmot riz and said: "I will not worry my red brothers with empty words! Let the Big Knives sing like mosquitos in the ears of the people! The Master of Life shall speak through the lips of

Striped Thunder. As for me, I bring no words, but a present to make your hearts glad!"

And I'm a Choctaw if he didn't rech down under a pile of robes and drag out Fat Bear's keg! I like to keeled over and I hear Fat Bear grunt like he'd been kicked in the belly. I seen Ondrey leering at me, and I instantly knowed he'd overheard us talking and had stole it out from amongst the hides after Fat Bear put it there for me. The way the braves' eyes glistened I knowed the Red-Coats had won, and I was licked.

Well, I war so knocked all of a heap, all I could think of was to out with my knife and git as many as I could before they got me. I aimed to git Sir Wilmot, anyway; they warn't enough men in the world to keep me from gutting him before I died. A Bearfield on his last rampage is wuss'n a cornered painter. You remember great-uncle Esau Bearfield. When the Creeks finally downed him, they warn't enough of 'em left alive in that war party to sculp him, and he was eighty-seven.

I reched for my knife, but jest then Sir Wilmot says: "Presently the milk of the Red-Coats will make the hearts of the warriors sing. But now is the time for the manifestations of the Great Spirit, whom the Sioux call Waukontonka, and other tribes other names, but he is the Master of Life for all. Let him speak through the lips of Striped Thunder."

So I thought I'd wait till everybody was watching the medicine lodge before I made my break. Striped Thunder went into the lodge and closed the flap, and the Socs lit fires in front of it and started dancing back and forth in front of 'em singing:

"Oh, Master of Life, enter the white skin lodge!

Possess him who sits within!

Speak through his mouth!"

I ain't going to mention what they throwed on the fires, but they smoked something fierce so you couldn't even see the lodge, and the Socs dancing back and forth looked like black ghosts. Then all to wunst they sounded a yell inside the lodge and a commotion like men fighting. The Injuns looked like they was about ready to rise up and go yonder in a hurry, but Sir Wilmot said: "Do not fear! The messenger of the Master of Life contends with the Unktehi for possession of the medicine man's body! Soon the good spirit will prevail and we will open the lodge and hear the words of Waukontonka!"

Well, hell, I knowed Striped Thunder wouldn't say nothing but jest what Sir Wilmot had told him to say; but them fool Injuns would believe they was gitting the straight goods from the Great Spirit hisself.

Things got quiet in the lodge and the smoke died down, and Sir Wilmot says: "Thy children await, O Waukontonka."

He opened the door, and I'm a Dutchman if they was anything in that lodge but a striped polecat!

He waltzed out with his tail h'isted over his back and them Injuns let out one arful yell and fell over backwards; and then they riz up and stampeded--Crows, Arikaras, Sioux, Socs and all, howling: "The Unktehi have prevailed! They have turned Striped Thunder into an evil beast!"

They didn't stop to open the gate. The Sioux clumb the stockade and the Crows busted right through it. I seen old Biting Hoss and Spotted Hawk leading the stampede, and I knowed the great Western Injun Confederation was busted all to hell. The women and chillern was right behind the braves, and in sight of fifteen seconds the only Injun in sight was Fat Bear.

Sir Wilmot jest stood there like he'd been putrified into rock, but Franswaw he run around behind the lodge and let out a squall. "Somebody's slit the back wall!" he howled. "Here's Striped Thunder lying behind the lodge with a knot on his head the size of a egg! Somebody crawled in and knocked him senseless and dragged him out while the smoke rolled!"

"The same man left the skunk!" frothed Sir Wilmot. "You Yankee dog, you're responsible for this!"

"Who you callin' a Yankee?" I roared, whipping out my knife.

"Remember the truce!" squalled Fat Bear, but Sir Wilmot was too crazy mad to remember anything. I parried his sword with my knife as he lunged, and grabbed his arm, and I reckon that was when he got his elber dislocated. Anyway he give a maddened yell and tried to draw a pistol with his good hand; so I hit him in the mouth with my fist, and that's when he lost them seven teeth he's so bitter about. Whilst he was still addled, I taken his pistol away from him and throwed him over the stockade. I got a idee his fractured skull was caused by him hitting his head on a stump outside. Meanwhile Ondrey and Franswaw was hacking at me with their knives, so I taken 'em by their necks and beat their fool heads together till they was limp, and then I throwed 'em over the stockade after Sir Wilmot.

"And I reckon that settles that!" I panted. "I dunno how this all come about, but you can call up yore women and chillern and tell 'em they're now citizens of the United States of America, by golly!"

I then picked up the keg, because I was hot and thirsty, but Fat Bear says: "Wait! Don't drink that! I--"

"Shet up!" I roared. "After all I've did for the nation tonight, I deserves a dram! Shame on you to begredge a old friend--"

I taken a big gulp--and then I give a maddened beller and throwed that keg as far as I could heave it, and run for water. I drunk about three gallons, and when I could breathe again I got a club and started after Fat Bear, who clumb up on top of a lodge.

"Come down!" I requested with passion. "Come down whilst I beats yore brains out! Whyn't you tell me what was in that keg?"

"I tried to," says he, "but you wouldn't listen. I thought it was whiskey when I stole it, or I wouldn't have taken it. I talked to Shingis while you were hunting the water bucket, jest now. It was him that put the skunk in the medicine lodge. He saw Ondrey hide the keg on Sir Wilmot's side of the council circle; he sneaked a drink out of it, and that's why he did what he did. It was for revenge. The onreasonable old buzzard thought Sir Wilmot was tryin' to pizen him."

So that's the way it was. Anyway, I'm quitting my job as soon as I git back to Saint Louis. It's bad enuff when folks gits too hifaluting to use candles, and has got to have oil lamps in a trading post. But I'll be derned if I'll work for a outfit which puts the whale-oil for their lamps in the same kind of kegs they puts their whiskey.

Your respeckful son.

Boone Bearfield.

THE END

www.ingramcontent.com/pod-product-compliance
Lightning Source LLC
Chambersburg PA
CBHW030244180626
46810CB00008B/3276